A Fire Truck for Chuck

Written by Annika Dunklee
Illustrated by Cathon

Owlkids Books

D_{UCK}.

D_{UCK}.

Fire truck.

"How much?"

"A buck."

What luck!
A fire truck
and for only
one buck.

Chuck and the fire truck.

The fire truck and Chuck.

Fire truck and Chuck
stuck in the muck.

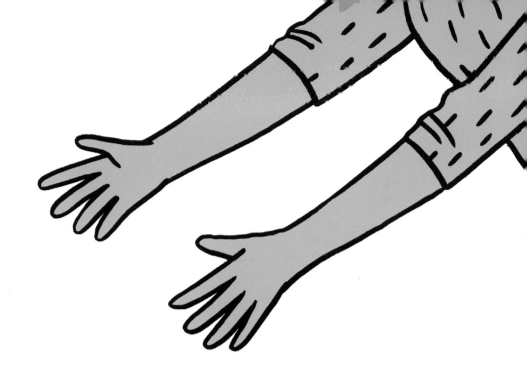

Fire truck and Chuck
plucked from the guck.

YUCK!

Hide and seek,
fire truck and Chuck!

Where is fire truck?

Where is Chuck?

Here's Chuck, but...

Fire truck under
the bed?
No…a mukluk.

Fire truck in
the hamper?
No…
a woodchuck.

Fire truck on the porch?
No, just…

Chuck is dumbstruck.
Where is fire truck?

"Wee-ou-wee-ou-wee-ou, *fire truck!*"

Chuck and fire truck
all tuckered out.

Tucking in fire truck.
Tucking in Chuck.

To Jack and John, and all the other little boys and girls who love fire trucks …even you! — A.D.

For my brother Samuel — C.

Cluck!

Text © 2018 Annika Dunklee
Illustrations © 2018 Cathon

Owlkids Books acknowledges the financial support of the Canada Council for the Arts, the Ontario Arts Council, the Government of Canada through the Canada Book Fund (CBF) and the Government of Ontario through the Ontario Media Development Corporation's Book Initiative for our publishing activities.

Published in Canada by
Owlkids Books Inc.
10 Lower Spadina Avenue
Toronto, ON M5V 2Z2

Published in the United States by
Owlkids Books Inc.
1700 Fourth Street
Berkeley, CA 94710

Cataloguing data available from Library and Archives Canada

Library of Congress Control Number: 2017943552

ISBN 978-1-77147-285-2 (hardcover)

The artwork in this book was created with a hand-drawn ink line and colored in Photoshop.
Edited by: Debbie Rogosin
Designed by: Danielle Arbour

ONTARIO ARTS COUNCIL
CONSEIL DES ARTS DE L'ONTARIO
an Ontario government agency
un organisme du gouvernement de l'Ontario

Canada Council
for the Arts

Conseil des Arts
du Canada

Canadä

Manufactured in Dongguan, China, in September 2017, by Toppan Leefung Packaging & Printing (Dongguan) Co., Ltd.
Job #BAYDC46

A   B   C   D   E   F

Owl kids | Publisher of Chirp, chickaDEE and OWL
www.owlkidsbooks.com | Owlkids Books is a division of  Bayard CANADA